FLORENCE PARRY HEIDE

Treehorn's Wish

DRAWINGS BY EDWARD GOREY

Holiday House New York

Library of Congress Cataloging in Publication Data

Heide, Florence Parry.
  Treehorn's wish.

  Summary: On his birthday Treehorn finds
a genie in a bottle and is granted the
standard of wishes.
  [1. Birthdays—Fiction]   I. Gorey, Edward,
1925-   , ill. II. Title.
PZ7.H36Tre 1983   [Fic]   83–6240
ISBN 0–8234–0493–5

EKA 2

For TED, with love

It was Treehorn's birthday.

The first thing he did was to make room for all the presents he might get. His parents hadn't given him very much the last few birthdays, so they were probably going to make up for it this time.

He put all of his socks and pajamas in his shirt drawer, so he'd have a place for some of the presents.

Then he cleared a big space in his closet by piling his piles of things on top of each other, so there was one big pile instead of a lot of little ones. That way, no matter how many presents he got, he'd have room for them.

Just before he went downstairs, he decided to push the chest of drawers over to the corner, out of the way, in case he got a television set of his own for his birthday.

Before he went downstairs, Treehorn called his friend Moshie.

"It's my birthday," said Treehorn.

"My birthday is the day after Christmas," said Moshie. "So I never get much. I hate having a birthday right after Christmas."

"I don't know what I'm going to get for mine," said Treehorn. "Maybe a television set of my own."

"Last year I got two games of Monopoly," said Moshie and hung up.

Treehorn went down to the kitchen. His mother was cleaning the refrigerator. All kinds of bottles and jars were on the kitchen counter. Treehorn didn't see any presents or a cake.

"It would be a shame to waste all these leftovers," said Treehorn's mother.

"It's my birthday," said Treehorn.

"So it is, dear," said his mother. "I wonder if we should have a cake or something. Maybe your father will see about it. Your prunes are on the table, Treehorn."

Treehorn sat down at the kitchen table. "I should make *some*thing with the leftovers," said Treehorn's mother. "Maybe a casserole. Or a salad of some kind. Maybe a nice aspic."

She started to put some of the jars back into the refrigerator.

Treehorn's father came into the kitchen.

"Do you know what today is, Treehorn?" he asked.

"Yes," said Treehorn. "It's my birthday."

"It's the first of the month," said Treehorn's father. "What does that mean to you?"

"It means presents and a birthday cake," said Treehorn.

"What the first of the month should mean to us is that it is the day we must pay our bills. Without fail, Treehorn, without fail. A man's credit is a man's honor."

"I have to get a new hat to go with my green suit," said Treehorn's mother. "Hats are coming back."

"I've just paid the bill for the suit, Emily," said Treehorn's father. "Can't we wait a while for the hat?"

"A suit isn't a suit without the right hat," said Treehorn's mother.

Treehorn started to eat his prunes.

"Emily, I'd like to go over some of these bills with you, if you don't mind," said Treehorn's father. "The gas bill is higher than it's ever been. There must be something wrong with the meter. I've called the company and asked them to send a meter reader over to the house this morning."

"I hope he comes pretty soon," said Treehorn's mother. "Before I go into town to buy my new hat."

"First things first," said Treehorn's father. "We'll have to go over the bills before we think of new hats. We have to know where our money goes, Emily."

Treehorn's mother and father went into the living room.

Treehorn wondered what presents they were going to give him for his birthday. Maybe a dog. Maybe there was a dog out in the yard right now. There might even be a pony. He'd never been allowed to have a pet before, but his parents might have changed their minds.

He walked out the back door. He didn't see a dog or a pony, but it looked as if someone had been digging a hole in the ground, so maybe there *was* a dog around somewhere.

He wondered what he would call the dog. If it was a white dog with black spots, he would call it Spot.

Treehorn walked over to the hole in the ground. It was just the kind of hole that a dog would dig if he was going to bury a bone or dig one up.

There was something in the hole. Treehorn reached in and lifted it out. It looked like some kind of jug. You never knew when you might need a jug, thought Treehorn, so he took it into the kitchen. It was covered with dirt. He'd have to clean it up.

His mother and father were still in the living room looking at the bills.

He spread yesterday's newspaper out on the kitchen table and set the jug on top of it. Then he took a rag from the cleaning closet. He sat down and started to clean the jug. A cork was in it, and he pulled it out.

There was a puff of smoke, and Treehorn saw that a very tall man with a bald head was standing in the kitchen. He was wearing big gold earrings and a long robe of some kind. He must be the meter reader.

"Where am I?" asked the man.

"In the kitchen," said Treehorn. "The meter is down in the basement."

The man rubbed his eyes and stretched. He didn't seem to be very interested in the basement.

Maybe he wasn't the meter reader at all, thought Treehorn. Maybe he was a genie. Treehorn had read a lot about genies. They lived in jugs or bottles until someone let them out. Maybe this genie had been in the jug that Treehorn had found in the backyard and he had got out when Treehorn took out the cork.

He didn't want to ask him if he was a genie, in case he was really a meter reader. He looked pretty sleepy. Maybe he was just bored. Reading meters must be kind of a boring job.

If he *was* a genie instead of a meter reader, then probably Treehorn would get three wishes. That was usually the way it worked with genies.

Treehorn decided to make a wish. That way he could tell whether the man was a genie or not.

"I wish I had a birthday cake," said Treehorn.

The man yawned and sat down at the kitchen table with Treehorn.

"There's a cake on the counter," he said.

Treehorn looked behind him. Sure enough, there *was* a cake.

It hadn't been there before, he was sure. Unless it had been there all along and he just hadn't noticed it, what with all the things from the refrigerator that had been on the counter.

Treehorn stood up and walked over to look at the cake. It said HAPPY BIRTHDAY. There were no candles.

There should be candles, thought Treehorn. That way you could make a wish when you blew them out.

"I wish there were some candles on the cake," said Treehorn.

"There *are* candles," said the man.

"No, there aren't," said Treehorn.

"Look again," said the man. Treehorn looked at the cake. There were candles on it now. He was sure there hadn't been any before.

Well, the man must be a genie, then. If he was, Treehorn had used up two of his wishes. One for the cake and one for the candles. Any genie he'd ever heard of granted only three wishes. He'd have to be pretty careful about the next wish. He wondered what it should be.

The genie leaned his head on the kitchen table and closed his eyes. He seemed to be dozing off.

"I should think it would be boring to stay in that jug all the time," said Treehorn.

"Not as boring as it is to get out," said the genie. "I can't get comfortable until I'm back in there. I hate having to come out and grant wishes to people I've never seen before. To people whose names I don't even know."

"My name is Treehorn," said Treehorn.

"Or want to know," the genie went on. "The truth is, I am very, very tired. If you don't mind, I'll just slip back into the jug for a little nap. As soon as I'm in, put the cork back so I don't drift out again while I'm asleep. When you're ready for your next wish, just take the cork out, all right?"

"All right," said Treehorn.

Treehorn watched as the genie sort of melted back into the jug. Treehorn put the cork in. Then he called his friend Moshie again.

"I found an old jug in the yard, and when I took out the cork a genie came out," he said. "I get three wishes. I wished for a cake and I got it."

"You could have wished for two cakes, you dumbbell," said Moshie, and hung up.

"I wished for a cake and I got it," said Treehorn.

"It's a very pretty cake, dear," said Treehorn's mother. "Wasn't it thoughtful of your father to remember to get it for you? Just remember our rule about eating sweets in the morning. You'll have to wait until tonight to have any cake."

"I get one more wish," said Treehorn. "I haven't decided what it should be yet. Maybe a television set."

"Your father and I are planning to watch a television program tonight," said Treehorn's mother. "It's about watching television, and whether people should. Maybe you'd like to see it with us."

Treehorn's father came back into the kitchen.

"Treehorn, I hope you've learned a good lesson by my example," he said. "The very moment I detected an increase in our gas bill, I telephoned the gas company to send their meter reader over to our home. Solve problems as they come along. That's the lesson I hope you have learned this morning."

"Look at my cake," said Treehorn.

What Moshie said was true, Treehorn decided. He *could* have wished for two cakes. He could have wished for a lot of cakes. He'd have to be more careful about his next wish. He didn't want to waste a perfectly good wish on anything dumb. Not that a cake was dumb, of course. A birthday isn't a birthday without a cake, Treehorn thought. And a cake isn't a birthday cake without candles.

Treehorn carried his cake over to the kitchen table and put it down next to the jug. It would have been nice to have had his name on the cake, but at least he had candles.

His mother came in and started to put the rest of the jars back in the refrigerator.

"I found this old jug in the backyard, and when I took out the cork a genie came out," said Treehorn.

"You know how your father and I feel about your bringing junk into the house," said Treehorn's mother. "You never know where it's been."

"It's a fine cake, and you're a lucky boy to have a mother who thinks of things like that," said Treehorn's father.

"I got it from a genie," said Treehorn. "I found a jug outside and I let the genie out of it. First I wished for a birthday cake, and then I wished for candles. Now I have only one wish left. I'm trying to make up my mind what it should be."

"You have to learn to make decisions, Treehorn," said his father. "We can't be wishy-washy."

"Chester, would you like a nice casserole tonight or an aspic?" asked Treehorn's mother.

"I don't know. Either one, dear," said Treehorn's father.

"I wish I hadn't used up two of my wishes already," said Treehorn.

"If something's worth wishing for, it's worth working for, my boy," said Treehorn's father.

"As soon as I decide what my next wish will be, I just have to let the genie out of the jug again," said Treehorn. "It's lucky I found it."

"We make our own luck," said Treehorn's father. "It only comes to those who work for it."

"I didn't have to work for it," said Treehorn. "I just went out to the yard and saw the jug. That's all there was to it. I didn't have to work at all."

"There is no substitute for work, Treehorn," said his father. "Working is its own reward."

"I could always make a nice lime aspic," said Treehorn's mother, looking into the refrigerator. "Lime is always nice. Such a good color."

"I'm going to the office now, Emily," said Treehorn's father. "Treehorn, remember our little lesson of the day. Solve your problems as you go along. And work, Treehorn. Work is the answer to everything."

"Or I could make a cream sauce, put all the leftovers in that," said Treehorn's mother.

After Treehorn's father had left for the office and Treehorn's mother had gone into the living room to dust, Treehorn picked up the jug. He felt like making a wish, but he wasn't sure what he wanted to wish for.

He could wish for a million dollars, but he wouldn't know where to put it. Even with all the extra space in his closet and bureau drawers, he wouldn't have enough room for a million dollars.

He could wish for a pony, but probably his parents wouldn't let him keep it. He could wish for his own television set, but it would probably be nicer than the one his parents had, and they'd want to trade with him.

There was a knock at the door, and Treehorn opened it.

"I'm supposed to take a look at your gas meter," said the man at the door.

"It's in the basement," said Treehorn. "See this jug? It's got a genie in it. The next time I take the cork out, I can make another wish."

"Look, it's not that I'm not interested in your jug and your genie, but I've got a job to do. If I stopped to listen to everyone who wanted to talk to me, I wouldn't get my job done, would I?"

He started down the basement stairs.

Treehorn looked at the jug. Maybe he could wish for another jug with another genie in it. That way he'd get three more wishes.

Treehorn's mother came in. "Did the meter reader come?" she asked.

"He's in the basement," said Treehorn.

"As soon as he's gone, we'll go into town, Treehorn. I'm going upstairs now to change into my green suit. That way I'll be sure that the new hat will match exactly."

"The genie got back into the jug. I can let him out when I decide what I want to wish," said Treehorn.

"That's nice, dear," said Treehorn's mother. "Be sure to wear your nice sweater when we go into town."

The doorbell rang. It was Treehorn's friend, Moshie.

"I came over to see what presents you got for your birthday," said Moshie.

"I didn't get any, but I'll probably get a lot of presents later," said Treehorn.

"Maybe and maybe not," said Moshie. "Last year all you got was that dumb sweater."

He walked over to look at the cake. "It should have your name on it," he said. "Otherwise it could be anybody's birthday cake. Is it chocolate? Chocolate makes me break out. If it's chocolate, I don't want any."

"I don't know what kind it is," said Treehorn. "I don't want to cut it until I've lit the candles and blown them out. That way I can have a wish."

The meter reader came up from the basement.

"How come you didn't put his name on his cake?" asked Moshie. "A birthday cake should have a name. No matter how stupid the name is, it should be on the cake."

The meter reader looked at Moshie. "I don't think I understand the question," he said.

"Let me see you get back in that jug if you're really a genie," said Moshie.

Treehorn's mother came in. She was wearing her green suit. "Are you the meter reader?" she asked. "Or are you the new friend that Treehorn was telling me about?"

"I'm the meter reader," said the meter reader. "Tell your husband there's nothing wrong with your meter. I've checked it out. Do you know that your children watch too much television? They are confusing fantasy with reality. Fact with fiction. That's a bad sign."

"I don't think you're much of a genie," said Moshie. "If you were a good one, you'd have put his name on the cake."

"See what I mean about your kids watching too much television?" asked the meter reader as he went out the door.

Moshie said,"I'm going, too. Call me if you get any presents."

"I do wish people wouldn't come to visit in the morning," said Treehorn's mother. "Especially on the days I'm cleaning the refrigerator. Or buying a new hat."

"I liked it when the genie came," said Treehorn.

"Afternoons are a much more suitable time for your friends to come over, Treehorn," said his mother. "Now get your sweater and we'll go into town to get my new hat. I do hope I can find the right green."

Treehorn went upstairs to get his sweater. It was the one his parents had given him for his birthday last year. He noticed that it was getting much too small.

He decided to take the jug along. That way he could let the genie out as soon as he thought of a good wish. He'd probably see something he wanted at the department store, and he could wish for it right away if he had the genie with him.

When Treehorn and his mother got to the store, they walked over to the elevator.

"Step all the way back in the car, please," said the elevator operator.

"There's a genie in this jug, and when I take the cork out I can make one more wish," Treehorn told him.

"You're lucky," said the elevator operator. "Nothing ever happens to me. No sweepstakes, no bingo, no door prizes. I never even found a four-leaf clover."

"I've already used up two wishes," said Treehorn.

"Second floor, draperies, sheets, towels," said the elevator operator. "I never even got the good part of a wishbone," he said.

"First I wished for a cake, and then I wished for candles," said Treehorn. "It would have been nice to have had my name on the cake, but at least it has candles."

"Third floor, millinery, scarves, and shoes," said the elevator operator. "I never even was lucky enough to find a comfortable pair of shoes."

"This is where we get off, Treehorn," said his mother.

"Wish me luck," said the elevator operator.

"Good luck," said Treehorn.

"That's easy for you to say," he said. "You've already got a jug with a genie in it."

Treehorn and his mother walked over to the hat department. A saleslady came over to them.

"May I help you?" she asked.

"I want to get a hat to match this green suit," said Treehorn's mother. "It has to be exactly the same shade of green. Exactly."

"It's a very unusual green. But don't worry, I'm sure we can find the right hat," said the saleslady. "There's always a right hat."

Treehorn's mother sat down in front of the mirror. Treehorn leaned against the wall, holding his jug.

"Straighten up, dear," said Treehorn's mother.

"You're a lucky boy to have a mother who cares," said the saleslady.

"And I'm lucky because there's a genie in this jug," said Treehorn. "As soon as I take the cork out, I get another wish. I can wish for anything I want."

"You couldn't wish for anything better than a mother who cares," said the saleslady. "As life goes by, you'll find that friends like your friend in the jug may come and go, but a mother's love lasts and lasts."

"I'm afraid it's going to be impossible to match the green," said Treehorn's mother.

"In this department, there's no such word as impossible," said the saleslady.

Treehorn wondered what wish he could make. He could wish for one of those big electric train sets. But maybe his parents were going to give him a train set for his birthday. He

didn't want to waste a wish on something he was going to get anyway.

"Now here's a lovely hat," said the saleslady. "Big brims are coming back this year."

"It's very nice," said Treehorn's mother. "But it's not the right green."

"It may not be the right green, but it's a very becoming hat," said the saleslady.

"But the green doesn't go," said Treehorn's mother. "I wanted the green to match *exactly.*"

The saleslady brought another hat. "Turbans are very popular this season," she said. "Turbans are really in."

"But it's a dreadful shade of green," said Treehorn's mother.

"Color isn't everything," said the saleslady. "Shape is the most important element in a hat. Shapes are coming back."

Treehorn's mother sighed. "I want a hat that's the same green as my suit," she said. "Exactly the same shade."

Treehorn thought that maybe he'd wish for a small electric car. It would look just like a regular car, only a little smaller. He wondered what color it should be.

"Now here's a hat that's exactly the right shade," said the saleslady.

Treehorn's mother looked in the mirror. "What an odd shape it is," she said.

"Odd shapes are in this year," said the saleslady.

"At least it's the right green," said Treehorn's mother. "I'll take it."

"You won't be sorry," said the saleslady. "The right hat makes all the difference."

Maybe he'd wish for an airplane, thought Treehorn. He could wish for an airplane pilot along with it. That way he could go anywhere he wanted. Anywhere in the world.

When they got home, Treehorn set the jug down on the kitchen counter. He still hadn't decided what he should wish for.

"Hang your sweater in your closet, Treehorn," said his mother. "Otherwise it will get out of shape."

Treehorn went upstairs to put his sweater in the closet. Now that he'd piled all of his piles of things in one pile, he did have a lot of extra room. Not enough for an airplane, of course, but enough for a lot of other things. And since he'd pushed his chest of drawers out of the way, he'd have plenty of room for the big electric train set, the one his parents might be giving him.

Treehorn came downstairs. His mother was standing at the kitchen counter in her green suit and her new hat. She picked up Treehorn's jug.

"I can't remember what's in here," she said. "It might be something I could add to the aspic." She pulled the cork out of the jug and set it on the counter.

There was a puff of smoke, and the genie stood in the kitchen. Treehorn's mother opened the refrigerator.

"All right, what's your wish?" asked the genie crossly. "Hurry up. I haven't got all day."

Treehorn wished he had more time to decide. He said, "I wish my name was on my birthday cake."

"It is," said the genie. "Now I have to find another jug. Tiresome, but that's the rule."

There was another puff of smoke, and the genie was gone.

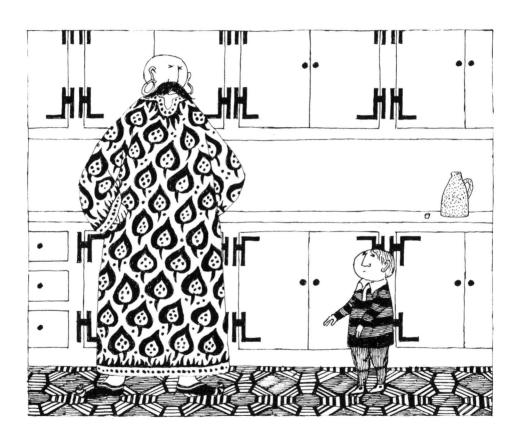

"I do wish your friends wouldn't come over at meal times, dear," said Treehorn's mother.

Treehorn's father came in from the dining room.

"How do you like my new hat, Chester?" asked Treehorn's mother. "It's very nice, dear," said Treehorn's father. "I'm sure it's very stylish."

"At the store I thought that it was the right green, but now I think it's a little off," said Treehorn's mother. "I wanted it to match my suit *exactly.*"

"All greens go together, dear," said Treehorn's father. "Just the way they do in nature."

"I've decided on the lime aspic," said Treehorn's mother.

"I used up all my wishes on my birthday cake," said Treehorn.

"It's a lovely cake," said Treehorn's mother. "And your father and I also have a very nice present for you."

She handed Treehorn a box. He opened it.

It was a sweater, just like Treehorn's old sweater, only bigger. The sleeves came down way below his hands. Well, he could always roll them up.

"It's a handsome sweater," said Treehorn's father, "and I'm sure you'll get a lot of wear out of it."

His parents went into the living room.

Treehorn walked over to the counter to look at his cake. Now it said, HAPPY BIRTHDAY TO TREEHORN. He carried it to the table.

Well, he'd had all his wishes, and now the genie was gone. Treehorn sat down at the kitchen table. He lit the candles on his birthday cake. Then he took a deep breath, made a wish, and blew out the candles.

There. He was sure his wish would come true. Even if it didn't, maybe he'd find another jug with another genie in it some day. Maybe even the same genie.

Anyway, he still had the cake. Treehorn pulled out the candles and started to cut the first piece.